permission or backing by the trademark owner. All trademarks and brands within this book are for clarifying purposes only and are owned by the owners themselves, not affiliated with this document.

# Aberto

**Type of Spell:** Charm

**Incantation:** Uh-bare-toe

**Purpose:** Used to open an object such as a chest, drawer, window, or door. However, it won't work if an object has been locked using an advanced spell!

**Casting Tips:** With your wand, point at the object you wish to open and say Aberto.


# Accio

**Type of Spell:** Charm

**Incantation:** AK-ee-oh or AK-see-oh

**Purpose:** Summons an object over short and long distances.

**Casting Tips:** Either summon the object by pointing at the object and saying the spell or by saying the spell then naming the object. For example, if you want to summon your TV remote to you while sitting down, you can point

your wand at the remote and say "Accio" or say "Accio TV remote".

# Age Line

**Type of Spell:** Charm

**Incantation:** Unknown

**Purpose.** Creates a boundary around an object that will now allow anyone over a set age to pass. Age potions won't work against this spell. The Weasley brothers have already tried!

**Casting Tips:** The incantation for this spell is unknown so you will either need to find an advanced spellbook in the restricted section of the library or ask Dumbledore.

# Aguamenti

**Type of Spell:** Conjuration

**Incantation:** AH-gwah-MEN-tee

**Purpose:** Shoots out a jet of water from the tip of your wand or creates a fountain of water in a basin.

**Casting Tips:** You have to visualize which of the two you want while chanting the spell.

# Alarte Ascendare

**Type of Spell:** Charm

**Incantation:** A-lar-tey Ah-sen-deh-ray

**Purpose:** Throws the target into the air. Smaller objects will go higher into the air than larger objects.

**Casting Tips:** With your wand, simply point at the object and say Alarte Ascendare. Remember that the larger and heavier the object, the more resistance you will feel on your wand so don't try this on anything too heavy!

# Alohomora

**Type of Spell:** Charm

**Incantation:** al-LOH-ha-MOHR-ah

**Purpose:** Locks and unlocks doors. It counters basic locking spells used to seal doors.

**Casting Tips:** As a beginner you will have to tap the door or lock once while casting the spell. Once you have gained enough practice, you should be able to simply point at the door and open it without any tapping.

# Anapneo

**Type of Spell:** Healing

**Incantation:** ah-NAP-nee-oh

**Purpose:** Clear's the animal or person's airway if it is blocked and they are having trouble breathing.

**Casting Tips:** This is a healing spell so it must be used with care. Be sure to correctly point your wand and say the spell clearly to ensure it is effective.

# Anteoculatia

**Type of Spell:** Hex

**Incantation:** AN-tea-oh-cuh-LAY-chee-a

**Purpose:** Transforms a person's hair into antlers.

**Casting Tips:** Be sure to turn the person's hair back to normal again by saying the spell once more!


# Anti-Cheating Spell

**Type of Spell:** Charm

**Incantation:** Unknown

**Purpose:** Prevents cheating while writing an exam. It is cast on parchment and quills.

**Casting Tips:** This spell is only known by the professors at Hogwarts and it is unknown how to reverse it. Therefore, be sure not to cheat on your tests!

# Aparecium

**Type of Spell:** Charm

**Incantation:** AH-par-EE-see-um

**Purpose:** Reverses concealing charms and invisible ink.

**Casting Tips:** If you are having trouble finding something or someone but are sure that something is missing, try using this spell. They may be hiding in plain sight using a concealment charm

# Appare Vestigium

**Type of Spell:** Charm

**Incantation:** app-PAH-ray vest-EE-gee-um

**Purpose:** Reveals footprints and tracking marks.

**Casting Tips:** Point at where footprints or a trail might be and cast this spell to reveal it.

# Apparate

**Type of Spell:** Teleportation

**Incantation:** aa-puh-ray-t

**Purpose:** Teleports you and anyone touching you to a location.

**Casting Tips:** Simply visualize the destination in your mind and say the spell. Remember that it must be a location that you have been to previously. This spell does not require a wand.

# Aqua Erecto

**Type of Spell:** Charm

**Incantation:** A-kwa ee-RUCK-toh

**Purpose:** Similar to Aguamenti but the jet of water produced is much stronger.

**Casting Tips:** The same as Aguamenti but remember that much more water is going to come out of your

wand. If a firefighter is secretly a wizard, you will be able to catch them using this spell.

# Arania Exumai

**Type of Spell:** Charm

**Incantation:** ah-RAHN-cc-a EKS-su-may

**Purpose:** Use this spell to blast away spiders.

**Casting Tips:** No need to fear spiders anymore once you know this spell. Simply point your wand at a spider or multiple spiders and chant the spell to blast them away.

# Arresto Momentum

**Type of Spell:** Charm

**Incantation:** ah-REST-oh mo-MEN-tum

**Purpose:**  Slows down a moving target. It can be used either on yourself or someone/something else.

**Casting Tips:**  Point your wand at either yourself or the target and say the spell to slow down. Great to cushion a fall!

# Ascendio

**Type of Spell:**  Charm

**Incantation:**  ah-SEN-dee-oh

**Purpose:**  Used to propel the caster into the air. Similar to Alarte Ascendare.

**Casting Tips:** Point your wand upwards and chant the spell for liftoff. You may go quite high into the air so be sure to use Arresto Momentum to fall down slowly!

# Avada Kedavra

**Type of Spell**: Unforgivable Curse

**Incantation**: ah-VAH-dah kah-DAV-rah

**Purpose**: One of the three Unforgivable Curses, meaning anyone who uses it automatically is to be imprisoned for life in Azkaban. Highly forbidden as it causes instant death to whoever it hits.

**Casting Tips**: This is an extremely forbidden curse and using it could get you locked up in Azkaban. If someone uses this on you, you have to counter it with another duelling spell such as Expelliarmus.

# Avifors

**Type of Spell**: Transfiguration

**Incantation**: AH-vi-fors

**Purpose**: Used to transform something or someone into a bird.

**Casting Tips**: This is quite a simple spell. Simply point your wand at the target and cast the spell. If used on a friend as a prank, be sure to transform them back!

# Avis

**Type of Spell**: Conjuration

**Incantation**: AH-viss

**Purpose**: Summons multiple birds from the tip of your wand.

**Casting Tips**: Be sure not to use this indoors or the birds will cause a mess. Use this conjuration spell outdoors!

# Baubillious

**Type of Spell**: Charm

**Incantation**: baw-BILL-ee-us

**Purpose:** A decoration charm used to cast ornaments onto an object.

**Casting Tips:** Great for decorating your Christmas tree easily. Simply point your wand at the tree and say the spell. Within seconds, the tree will be beautifully decorated.

# Bewitched Snowballs

**Type of Spell:** Charm

**Incantation:** Unknown

**Purpose:** Causes snowballs to automatically throw themselves at a target.

**Casting Tips:** This is a spell that pranksters love to use. Ask any prankster wizard if they know the incantation or ask the Weasley twins!

# Bombarda

**Type of Spell**: Charm

**Incantation**: bom-BAR-dah

**Purpose**: Causes a small explosion at the location the wand is pointed at.

**Casting Tips**: This is a potentially dangerous spell due to its explosive nature. Be sure to only use it where it is safe to do so.

# Bombarda Maxima

**Type of Spell**: Charm

**Incantation**: BOM-bar-dah MAX-ih-mah

**Purpose**: An amplified version of Bombarda that causes a bigger explosion.

**Casting Tips**: Similar to Bombarda, be sure to use this only when safe to do so.

# Brackium Emendo

**Type of Spell**: Healing Spell

**Incantation**: BRA-key-um ee-MEN-doh

**Purpose**: Heals broken bones

**Casting Tips**: Be sure to pronounce the incantation correctly otherwise the bones will vanish and you will be left with a body part that is like rubber.


# Bubble Head Charm

**Type of Spell**: Charm

**Incantation**: Unknown

**Purpose**: Covers the mouth and nose with a bubble, allowing you to breathe underwater.

**Casting Tips**: The incantation for this spell is unknown but Cedric Digory may know it since he has used it before!

# Calvario

**Type of Spell**: Curse

**Incantation**: cal-VORE-ee-oh

**Purpose**: Causes hair loss on the target.

**Casting Tips**: Be sure to give the target a hair growth potion afterwards!


# Cantis

**Type of Spell**: Jinx

**Incantation**: CAN-tiss

**Purpose**: Makes the target start singing uncontrollably.

**Casting Tips**: Great for your shy friends on karaoke nights!

# Carpe Retractum

**Type of Spell**: Conjuration

**Incantation**: CAR-pay ruh-TRACK-tum

**Purpose**: Conjures a magical rope from the tip of your wand and propels it towards a target to pull it towards you.

**Casting Tips**: Move your wand above your head in a circular motion like you are a cowboy throwing a lasso then chant the spell and point your wand at the target.


# Cave Inimicum

**Type of Spell**: Charm

**Incantation**: KAH-way ih-NIH-mih-kum

**Purpose**: Sets off a loud noise if intruders are approaching.

**Casting Tips**: Use the spell far from whatever you are trying to protect so that you have lots of time to escape or prepare for the intruders.

# Cistem Aperio

**Type of Spell:** Charm

**Incantation:** SIS-tem uh-PEH-ree-o

**Purpose:** Opens chests and boxes.

**Casting Tips:** This is similar to Aberto but only works on chests and boxes. If Aberto doesn't work, try this spell.

# Colloportus

**Type of Spell:** Charm

**Incantation:** cul-loh-POR-tus

**Purpose:** Locking spell.

**Casting Tips:** This spell is easily countered by Alohomora.

# Colloshoo

**Type of Spell:** Hex

**Incantation:** cul-loh-SHOE

**Purpose:** Conjures stick glue underneath the target's shoes which can cause them to trip or be glued to the floor.

**Casting Tips:** Be sure to point your wand at the target's shoes otherwise the spell won't work properly. Also, be prepared for a mess!

# Colovaria

**Type of Spell:** Charm

**Incantation:** co-loh-VAH-riah

**Purpose:** Changes an object's color.

**Casting Tips:** Great for decorating.

# Confringo

**Type of Spell**: Curse

**Incantation**: kon-FRING-goh

**Purpose**: Explodes the target and makes it burst in flames.

**Casting Tips**: Like Bombarda, this is a dangerous spell so be sure to only practice this in an open area.

# Confundo

**Type of Spell**: Charm

**Incantation**: con-FUN-doh

**Purpose**: Confuses and disorients the target.

**Casting Tips**: Make sure not to use this on someone driving!

# Conjunctivitus

**Type of Spell:** Curse

**Incantation:** con-junct-uh-vite-us

**Purpose:** Temporarily blinds the target.

**Casting Tips:** An anti blinding potion may be needed if the target's vision does not come back.


# Crinus Muto

**Type of Spell:** Charm

**Incantation:** cry-NUS moo-toh

**Purpose:** Changes the color and/or style of the target's hair.

**Casting Tips:** Can be used on yourself or someone else. Image the style and color you want and cast the spell while pointing your wand at the target. Great to use on yourself if you are late for school or work!

# Crucio

**Type of Spell**: Unforgivable Curse

**Incantation**: crew-SHEE-oh

**Purpose**: Another one of the Unforgivable Curses which inflicts great pain on the target. The pain is said to feel like being stabbed with multiple hot knives.

**Casting Tips**: This spell cannot be used normally by chanting. The caster must actually want to inflict great pain on the target for this spell to be cast.


# Defodio

**Type of Spell**: Charm

**Incantation**: deh-FOH-dee-oh

**Purpose**: Used to carve through stone or on the ground.

**Casting Tips**: This spell is great for engraving messages.

# Deletrius

**Type of Spell**:  Charm

**Incantation**:  deh-LEE-tree-us

**Purpose**:  Erases the shadow of a previous spell.

**Casting Tips**: Great for destroying Voldemort's Dark Mark if you ever see it in the sky.


# Densaugeo

**Type of Spell**:  Hex/Healing Spell

**Incantation**:  den-SAW-jee-oh

**Purpose**:  Causes the target's teeth to grow rapidly.

**Casting Tips**:  This can be used as either a hex or a healing spell. If someone's teeth are in good condition, then these will cause them to grow beyond normal. However, if someone has lost teeth due to an incident then it will help regrow them quickly.

# Depulso

**Type of Spell:** Counter Charm

**Incantation:** deh-PUL-soh

**Purpose:** This spell is the opposite of Accio in that it causes the target to propel away from the caster to a specified location.

**Casting Tips:** Be sure to use Arresto Momentum with this if used on someone so they don't get hurt!


# Descendo

**Type of Spell:** Charm

**Incantation:** deh-SEN-doh

**Purpose:** Propels a target object or person downwards.

**Casting Tips:** Be sure to move your wand in a downward motion when casting this spell. The faster the movement, the faster the target will move downwards.

# Deprimo

**Type of Spell**: Charm

**Incantation**: DEE-prih-moh

**Purpose**: Places intense downward pressure on a location or object.

**Casting Tips**: Unlike descend, you don't need to move your wand downwards with this spell.


# Diffindo

**Type of Spell**: Charm

**Incantation**: dih-FIN-doh

**Purpose**: Can be used to tear or rip through a target.

**Casting Tips**: Use this to forcefully open bags or any other soft material.

# Diminuendo

**Type of Spell**:  Charm

**Incantation**:  dim-in-YEW-en-DOUGH

**Purpose**:  Shrinks the target object or person.

**Casting Tips**: Be careful not to step on the person once you've shrank them!


# Dissendium

**Type of Spell**:  Charm

**Incantation**:  dih-SEN-dee-um

**Purpose**:  Used to open secret passageways.

**Casting Tips**:  Try this spell if the other unlocking spells don't work.

# Draconifors

**Type of Spell:** Configuration

**Incantation:** drah-KOH-nih-fors

**Purpose:** Turns the target into a dragon.

**Casting Tips:** A dragon is a very dangerous creature. Be careful when using this spell and watch out for that fiery breath.


# Ducklifors

**Type of Spell:** Transfiguration

**Incantation:** DUCK-lih-fors

**Purpose:** Turns the target into a duck.

**Casting Tips:** Thankfully, ducks are much less dangerous than dragons so no need to worry about any fire breathing with this spell.

# Duro

**Type of Spell:** Charm

**Incantation:** DOO-roh

**Purpose:** Turns the target into stone.

**Casting Tips:** Remember to transform the person back!


# Ebublio

**Type of Spell:** Jinx

**Incantation:** ee-BUB-lee-oh

**Purpose:** Causes an object to explode into bubbles.

**Casting Tips:** Much more efficient than using a bubble wand!

# Engorgio

**Type of Spell**: Charm

**Incantation**: en-GOR-jee-oh

**Purpose**: Makes the target inflate in size.

**Casting Tips**: No need to order large sizes for pizza anymore. Use this spell to make every pizza a large!


# Engorgio Skullus

**Type of Spell**: Charm

**Incantation**: in-GORE-jee-oh SKUH-las

**Purpose**: Same as Engorgio but specifically used to inflate someone's head.

**Casting Tips**: Unfortunately this spell can't be used for pizzas.

# Entomorphis

**Type of Spell**: Transfiguration

**Incantation**: en-TOE-morph-iss

**Purpose**: Turns the target into an insect for a short period of time.

**Casting Tips**: Be careful not to step on it by accident!


# Episkey

**Type of Spell**: Healing Spell

**Incantation**: ee-PISS-key

**Purpose**: Heals moderately severe injuries such as broken bones and cuts.

**Casting Tips**: This spell will save a lot of trips to the hospital.

# Epoximase

**Type of Spell:** Charm

**Incantation:** ee-POX-i-mise

**Purpose:** Used to glue things together.

**Casting Tips:** This spell will save the sticky mess that you get from using glue.


# Erecto

**Type of Spell:** Charm

**Incantation:** eh-RECK-toh

**Purpose:** Erects structures.

**Casting Tips:** Great for camping when you need to setup a tent.

# Evanesce

**Type of Spell:** Charm

**Incantation:** ev-an-ES-key

**Purpose:** Makes the target temporarily invisible.

**Casting Tips:** Become a hide and go seek champion with this spell.


# Evanesco

**Type of Spell:** Charm

**Incantation:** ev-an-ES-koh

**Purpose:** An alternative to Evanesce.

**Casting Tips:** If you don't have an Invisibility Cloak, then these spells can be used in the meantime.

# Everte Statum

**Type of Spell:** Charm

**Incantation:** ee-VER-tay STAH-tum

**Purpose:** Launches the target backwards.

**Casting Tips:** Push your wand forwards as you cast the spell. The faster you push forward, the greater the force of the spell.


# Expecto Patronum

**Type of Spell:** Charm

**Incantation:** ecks-PECK-toh pah-TROH-num

**Purpose:** A defensive spell that uses happy memories and emotions to create a spell that can drive away Dementors and Lethifolds.

**Casting Tips:** Make a list of the top 2-3 happiest memories in your life and focus on channelling those memories. The more positive emotion you are able to feel while casting the spell, the stronger your Patronus

will be. Eventually, you will be able to cast a Patronus that will take the form of something important to you which is the highest level of the Patronus charm.

# Expelliarmus

**Type of Spell:** Charm

**Incantation:** ex-PELL-ee-ARE-muss

**Purpose:** Disarms an opponent by knocking out whatever is in their hand. It can also knock out someone if used with too much force.

**Casting Tips:** As you are saying the incantation, flick your wand forward. The greater the force in the flick of the hand, the more force the spell will have.

# Expulso

**Type of Spell**: Curse

**Incantation**: ecks-PUHL-soh

**Purpose**: Very similar to Bombarda in that it produces an explosion but Expulso's is produced with pressure rather than heat.

**Casting Tips**: Similar to Bombarda. Be sure to only use this when safe to do so!

# Ferula

**Type of Spell**: Healing Spell

**Incantation**: feh-ROO-lah

**Purpose**: Produces a splint and a bandage typically used for healing broken bones.

**Casting Tips**: This is a more appropriate spell to use if Muggles are around you and will arouse less suspicion than other healing spells.

# Fianto Duri

**Type of Spell:** Charm

**Incantation:** fee-AN-toh DOO-ree

**Purpose:** A defensive spell used to make shield spells stronger.

**Casting Tips:** Sometimes a good defense is just as important as a good offense so make sure to remember this spell.


# Fidelius Charm

**Type of Spell:** Charm

**Incantation:** fid-DELL-ee-us

**Purpose:** Hides secrets within the target who becomes a Secret-Keeper. The secret becomes impossible to find unless the Secret-Keeper chooses to release it.

**Casting Tips:** Be sure that Secret-Keeper is someone who can be fully trusted.

# Finestra

**Type of Spell:** Curse

**Incantation:** fi-Ness-Trah

**Purpose:** Creates an opening in a wall.

**Casting Tips:** You may find yourself using doors a lot less after using this spell.

# Finite

**Type of Spell:** Counter Spell

**Incantation:** fi-NEE-tay

**Purpose:** Gets rid of spell effects close to the caster.

**Casting Tips:** Point your wand high in the air while casting to maximize the area of the spell.

# Finite Incantatem

**Type of Spell**: Counter Spell

**Incantation**: fi-NEE-tay in-can-TAH-tem

**Purpose**: Produces the same effect as Finite except with a larger area of effect.

**Casting Tips**: Same as Finite.

---

# Firestorm

**Type of Spell**: Charm

**Incantation**: Fye-er storm

**Purpose**: Generates a large amount of fire from the tip of the wand.

**Casting Tips**: As with any fire spell be sure to do this only in an area where someone can't get hurt! The more emotion you put into this spell, the greater the intensity of the fire.

# Flagrate

**Type of Spell:** Charm

**Incantation:** fluh-GRAH-tay

**Purpose:** Can be used to write on walls with fiery writing with the wand acting as the quill.

**Casting Tips:** Be sure to have your wand pointed at the correct wall before saying the incantation!


# Flipendo

**Type of Spell:** Jinx

**Incantation:** flih-PEN-doh

**Purpose:** Knocks the target back but may knock out weaker enemies.

**Casting Tips:** The harder you push your wand forward while casting this spell, the harder the knockback.

# Flipendo Tria

**Type of Spell**: Jinx

**Incantation**: flih-PEN-doh TREE-ah

**Purpose**: A stronger version of Flipendo.

**Casting Tips**: Has the ability of casting a mini tornado. Typically Flipendo is enough to get the task done.

# Fumos

**Type of Spell**: Charm

**Incantation**: Few-mos

**Purpose**: Produces a light smokescreen.

**Casting Tips**: Perfect for escaping.

# Fumos Duo

**Type of Spell**: Charm

**Incantation**: Few-mos Dew-o

**Purpose**: Produces a heavy smokescreen.

**Casting Tips**: Normally Fumos will be enough concealment to escape but should you be needing more, this spell should do the trick.

# Furnunculus

**Type of Spell**: Jinx

**Incantation**: fer-NUN-kyoo-luss

**Purpose**: Covers the target's skin in pimples and boils.

**Casting Tips**: Where you point your wand while chanting the spell is area that will be affected. Great for pranks but be sure to give them the correct potion afterwards!

# Geminio

**Type of Spell**: Curse

**Incantation**: jeh-MIH-nee-oh

**Purpose**: Creates an unfunctional copy of a person or object.

**Casting Tips**: Cannot be used on gold as the Ministry of Magic has precautions in place to detect the copies.

# Glacius

**Type of Spell**: Charm

**Incantation**: GLAY-shuss

**Purpose**: Turns the target into ice.

**Casting Tips**: Since ice will break on impact and/or melt, be sure to turn the target back and be careful when using this spell in hot weather!

# Glacius Tria

**Type of Spell:** Charm

**Incantation:** GLAY-shuss TREE-ah

**Purpose:** A stronger version of Glacius. Keeps the target frozen for longer.

**Casting Tips:** Same as Glacius.


# Glisseo

**Type of Spell:** Charm

**Incantation:** GLISS-ee-oh

**Purpose:** Transforms stairs into a slide.

**Casting Tips:** Stairs will be much more fun to use but be sure to turn them back to stairs by chanting the spell again and tapping with your wand.

# Harmonia Nectere Passus

**Type of Spell:** Charm

**Incantation:** har-MOH-nee-a NECK-teh-ray PASS-us

**Purpose:** Repairs broken objects.

**Casting Tips:** If something gets broken beyond repair then this spell most likely will not work.

# Herbivicus

**Type of Spell:** Charm

**Incantation:** her-BIV-i-cuss

**Purpose:** Causes plants to grow to their full size instantly.

**Casting Tips:** Be sure to follow your wand upwards as the plant grows or the spell will be incomplete.

# Homenum Revelio

**Type of Spell:** Charm

**Incantation:** HOM-eh-num reh-VEH-lee-oh

**Purpose:** Reveals if any humans, including wizards, are nearby.

**Casting Tips:** This can be used to detect people hiding under invisibility spells or cloaks too.


# Homorphus

**Type of Spell:** Charm

**Incantation:** Ho-MOR-fuss

**Purpose:** Reverts an Animagus or transformed object back to its original state.

**Casting Tips:** Remember this spell when going through a forest. You may need it if a werewolf appears!

# Horcrux

**Type of Spell**: Curse

**Incantation**: Unknown.

**Purpose**: Splits a part of the user's soul into an object. However, in order to do this, one must commit murder which allows the soul to be ripped. Due to the deep dark nature of the curse, it is known to very few wizards.

**Casting Tips**: Strictly forbidden.


# Hot Air Charm

**Type of Spell**: Charm

**Incantation**: Unknown

**Purpose**: Emits hot air from the tip of the wand.

**Casting Tips**: Most common use of this spell is to dry one's clothes.

# Hour Reversal Charm

**Type of Spell**: Charm

**Incantation**: Unknown

**Purpose**: Reverses time up to 5 hours.

**Casting Tips**: This is an extremely unstable charm therefore it should be used minimally and with caution.


# Hurling Hex

**Type of Spell**: Hex

**Incantation**: Unknown

**Purpose**: Causes your broom to shake violently and attempt to throw you off.

**Casting Tips**: If you notice your broom is acting strange, especially in a quidditch match, your broom most likely has been hexed by another wizard.

# Illegibilus

**Type of Spell:** Charm

**Incantation:** i-lej-i-bill-us

**Purpose:** Makes any text illegible.

**Casting Tips:** Very useful if you have a journal so no one can read it.


# Immobulus

**Type of Spell:** Charm

**Incantation:** eem-o-bue-les or ihm-o-bue-luss

**Purpose:** Immobilizes the target.

**Casting Tips:** Only works on living things.

# Impedimenta

**Type of Spell**: Charm

**Incantation**: im-ped-ih-MEN-tah

**Purpose**: Impedes movement of the target.

**Casting Tips**: This spell can be used in many ways. For example, if there is something on the ground where the target is running, then that object may be used to trip the target. If nothing is available, then the spell will simply push back the target with force.

# Imperio

**Type of Spell**: Unforgivable Curse

**Incantation**: im-PEER-ee-oh

**Purpose**: Another one of the three Unforgivable Curses. Puts the target in a hypnotic state and conforms them to the user's will.

**Casting Tips**: By building enough willpower and practicing, you can learn how to resist this curse.

# Impervius

**Type of Spell**:  Charm

**Incantation**:  im-PER-vee-us

**Purpose**:  Makes the target impervious to a specific substance.

**Casting Tips**:  For example, if you leave something out in the rain but charm it against the rain then it won't get wet.

# Inanimatus Conjuras

**Type of Spell**:  Conjuration

**Incantation**:  in-an-ih-MAH-tus CON-jur-us

**Purpose:** Creates an inanimate object.

**Casting Tips:** The clearer the object is in your mind, the better it will turn out from the spell.

# Incarcerous

**Type of Spell:** Charm

**Incantation:** in-CAR-ser-us

**Purpose:** Ties up the target using charmed ropes.

**Casting Tips:** Spin the wand in a circular motion around the target. The faster you move your wand, the tighter the ropes will be bound.

# Incendio

**Type of Spell:** Charm

**Incantation:** in-SEN-dee-oh

**Purpose:** Makes a small fire.

**Casting Tips:** The angrier you are, the more intense the flame that will be produced.


# Incendio Duo

**Type of Spell:** Charm

**Incantation:** in-SEN-dee-oh DOO-oh

**Purpose:** More powerful version of Incendio

**Casting Tips:** Anger also channels this spell. Be careful with this spell or you may cause a disaster.

# Inflatus

**Type of Spell:** Charm

**Incantation:** in-FLAY-tus

**Purpose:** Inflates objects. Different from just simply increasing their size.

**Casting Tips:** Simply point your wand at the target and incantate the spell.


# Lacarnum Inflamarae

**Type of Spell:** Charm

**Incantation:** la-CAR-num in-fla-MA-ray

**Purpose:** Sends a ball of fire from the tip of the wand.

**Casting Tips:** Similar to the other fire spells, the angrier you are, the larger and hotter the ball of fire will be.

# Locomotor Wibbly

**Type of Spell**: Jinx

**Incantation**: loh-koh-MOH-tor WIB-lee

**Purpose**: Puts the targets legs to sleep effectively immobilizing them.

**Casting Tips**: Be sure to aim your wand at the target's legs.

# Langlock

**Type of Spell**: Jinx

**Incantation**: LANG-lock

**Purpose**: Glues the target's tongue to the roof their mouth.

**Casting Tips**: Point towards the mouth of the target and flick your wand upwards as you say the incantation.

# Lapifors

**Type of Spell**: Transfiguration

**Incantation**: LAP-ih-forz

**Purpose**: Transforms the target into a rabbit.

**Casting Tips**: Chanting lapifors again while tapping the rabbit with your wand will transform the target back into its original object.

# Legilimens

**Type of Spell**: Charm

**Incantation**: Le-JIL-ih-mens

**Purpose**: Allows you to see into the memories, thoughts, and emotions of the target.

**Casting Tips**: This spell is only to be used with the target's permission.

# Levicorpus

**Type of Spell**: Jinx

**Incantation**: lev-ee-CORE-pus

**Purpose**: Dangles the target by their ankles and upside down.

**Casting Tips**: Points towards the targets ankles as you chant the spell.

# Liberacorpus

**Type of Spell**: Counter Spell

**Incantation**: LIB-er-ah-cor-pus

**Purpose**: Used to counter the effects of Levicorpus.

**Casting Tips**: While the target is danling, say this spell and they will be dropped down.

# Locomotor

**Type of Spell**: Charm

**Incantation**: LOH-koh-moh-tor

**Purpose**: Causes an object to animate and start moving around.

**Casting Tips**: Careful when casting on large objects as they can cause quite the mess!


# Locomotor Mortis

**Type of Spell**: Curse

**Incantation**: LOH-koh-moh-tor MOR-tis

**Purpose**: Locks the targets legs together.

**Casting Tips**: The faster the wand is waved, the tighter the legs will lock.

# Lumos

**Type of Spell:** Charm

**Incantation:** LOO-mos

**Purpose:** Emits some light from the tip of your wand.

**Casting Tips:** No need for a flashlight from now. You can control the brightness of the light using your off hand. Raising it up will increase the brightness and lowering it will decrease the brightness.

# Lumos Duo

**Type of Spell:** Charm

**Incantation:** LOO-mos DOO-oh

**Purpose:** Creates a more intense light than Lumos.

**Casting Tips:** Same as lumos.

# Lumos Maxima

**Type of Spell:** Charm

**Incantation:** LOO-mos Ma-cks-ima

**Purpose:** The strongest version of Lumos.

**Casting Tips:** The intense ball of light can be thrown by swinging your wand. Guard your eyes when using this or it may damage your eyes.

# Lumos Solem

**Type of Spell:** Charm

**Incantation:** LOO-mos SO-lem

**Purpose:** Emits a ray of light that projects forward rather than just at the tip of the wand like Lumos.

**Casting Tips:** Point your wand at where you want the ray of light to go.

# Magicus Extremos

**Type of Spell**: Charm

**Incantation**: maj-ik-us eks-treem-os

**Purpose**: All spells in the vicinity of the caster become more powerful.

**Casting Tips**: Remember that both your spells and your opponent's spells will become stronger.

# Melofors

**Type of Spell**: Jinx

**Incantation**: mel-o-fours

**Purpose**: Puts a pumpkin on the target's head.

**Casting Tips**: Be sure to point your wand at their head when casting. A great prank during Halloween.

# Meteolojinx Recanto

**Type of Spell:** Counter Spell

**Incantation:** mee-tee-OH-loh-jinks reh-CAN-toh

**Purpose:** Reverses the effects of all weather effects caused by a jinx.

**Casting Tips:** If you are having bad weather, try casting this spell to see if it goes away but be careful of the lighting!

# Mimblewimble

**Type of Spell:** Curse

**Incantation:** MIM-bull-WIM-bull

**Purpose:** Prevents the target from letting out a secret by twisting their tongue whenever they try to reveal it.

**Casting Tips:** Whisper the secret you are referring to then cast the spell.

# Mobiliarbus

**Type of Spell:** Charm

**Incantation:** MO-bil-ee-AR-bus

**Purpose:** Allows the caster to levitate and move objects.

**Casting Tips:** The heavier the object, the more downward force you will feel on your wand. Therefore, there are certain objects you will not be able to levitate.

# Mobilicorpus

**Type of Spell:** Charm

**Incantation:** MO-bil-ee-COR-pus

**Purpose:** A sister spell to Mobiliarbus except that it only works on bodies.

**Casting Tips:** Mobiliarbus is a better spell to learn out of the two since it can be used for more objects.

# Morsmordre

**Type of Spell**: Curse

**Incantation**: morz-MOR-drah

**Purpose**: Casts the Dark Mark, the symbol of Voldemort's Death Eaters.

**Casting Tips**: If this spell is cast, it means that Voldemort and his Death Eaters are close by. Warn your allies!


# Muffliato

**Type of Spell**: Charm

**Incantation**: muf-lee-AH-to

**Purpose**: Dulls the target's hearing to prevent them from eavesdropping.

**Casting Tips**: While casting, flick your wand at both the target's ears otherwise only one ear will be dulled.

# Multicorfors

**Type of Spell**: Transfiguration

**Incantation**: mull-tee-COR-fors

**Purpose**: Changes the color of an object.

**Casting Tips**: Color coordinating your outfits will be much easier with this spell!

# Nox

**Type of Spell**: Counter Charm

**Incantation**: Nocks

**Purpose**: Turns off Lumos.

**Casting Tips**: Chanting Lumos two times won't turn off Lumos. This spell must be used.

# Nebulus

**Type of Spell:** Charm

**Incantation:** NEH-bu-lus

**Purpose:** Fog is created from the tip of the wand.

**Casting Tips:** This spell takes about 2 minutes for enough fog to be created.

# Oculus Reparo

**Type of Spell:** Charm

**Incantation:** awk-yu-luss ruh-pair-o

**Purpose:** Fixes broken glasses.

**Casting Tips:** No more expensive bills from the optical store once you learn this spell!

# Obliviate

**Type of Spell**: Charm

**Incantation**: oh-BLI-vee-ate

**Purpose**: Erases a person's memory about a specific event.

**Casting Tips**: This is a must know for every wizard in case a Muggle sees you use magic. Casting this spell on them will make them forget what they saw which will save you a meeting with the Ministry of Magic.

# Obscuro

**Type of Spell**: Conjuration

**Incantation**: ob-SKYOOR-oh

**Purpose**: Conjures a blindfold around the target's eyes.

**Casting Tips**: Be sure to aim at the target's eyes or the blindfold won't wrap around their eyes.

# Oppugno

**Type of Spell**: Jinx

**Incantation**: oh-PUG-noh

**Purpose**: Turns animals and lesser creature aggressive causing them to attack an opponent.

**Casting Tips**: Point first at the animal or being then at the target while casting the spell to direct the aggression.


# Orbis

**Type of Spell**: Jinx

**Incantation**: OR-biss

**Purpose**: Creates a hole in the ground.

**Casting Tips**: No more need for shovels!

# Orchideous

**Type of Spell**: Conjuration

**Incantation**: or-KID-ee-us

**Purpose**: Conjures a bouquet of flowers

**Casting Tips**: This will save a lot of money on Valentine's day!

# Pack

**Type of Spell**: Charm

**Incantation**: Pak

**Purpose**: Packs up your luggage for you.

**Casting Tips**: While chanting the spell, point at all the objects you want packed then point at the luggage in which you want to put it in.

# Partis Temporus

**Type of Spell:** Charm

**Incantation:** PAR-tis temp-OAR-us

**Purpose:** Produces an opening to pass through protective magical barriers.

**Casting Tips:** Moving your wand in a larger motion will create a bigger opening.


# Periculum

**Type of Spell:** Charm

**Incantation:** purr-ICK-you-lum

**Purpose:** Shoots out red flares and sparks from the tip of your wand.

**Casting Tips:** This is a great spell for letting someone know of your location.

# Peskipiksi Pesternomi

**Type of Spell:** Charm

**Incantation:** PES-key PIX-ee PES-ter NO-mee

**Purpose:** Used by Gilderoy Lockhart to get rid of Cornish Pixies but had no effect.

**Casting Tips:** Like Gilderoy Lockhart himself, this spell is most likely a fake.

# Petrificus Totalus

**Type of Spell:** Curse

**Incantation:** pe-TRI-fi-cus to-TAH-lus

**Purpose:** Binds the target's body in an immobile state with their hands glued to their hips. The target will end up falling to the ground.

**Casting Tips:** Be sure to use Arresto Momentum as well to cushion the target's fall.

# Piertotum Locomotor

**Type of Spell**: Charm

**Incantation**: pee-ayr-TOH-tum loh-koh-MOH-tor

**Purpose**: Animates inanimate objects such as statues and makes them subject to the will of the caster.

**Casting Tips**: Remember that some of these objects are fragile so be careful with what you assign them or they may break.

# Point Me

**Type of Spell**: Charm

**Incantation**: N/A

**Purpose**: Makes your wand act as a compass with the tip of the wand pointing north.

**Casting Tips**: Perfect for anywhere you don't have a signal for your phone and can't use a Maps app.

# Portus

**Type of Spell:** Charm

**Incantation:** POR-tus

**Purpose:** Transforms any object into a port-key.

**Casting Tips:** A port-key can teleport you to a specific location that you imagine in your mind.


# Prior Incantato

**Type of Spell:** Charm

**Incantation:** pri-OR in-can-TAH-toh

**Purpose:** Shows what spell was last cast from a wand.

**Casting Tips:** Typically used by detectives from the Ministry of Magic during an investigation.

# Protego

**Type of Spell:** Charm

**Incantation:** pro-TAY-goh

**Purpose:** Reflects and neutralizes minor to moderate spells from the attacker.

**Casting Tips:** This will not work on powerful spells such as Avada Kedavra.

# Protego Horribilis

**Type of Spell:** Charm

**Incantation:** pro-TAY-goh horr-uh-BIHL-ihs

**Purpose:** A variation of Protego that can protect against more powerful Dark Magic spells than Protego can.

**Casting Tips:** Be sure to use this spell rather than Protego when dealing with a Dark Wizard.

# Protego Maxima

**Type of Spell:** Charm

**Incantation:** pro-TAY-goh MAX-ee-Ma

**Purpose:** The most powerful variation of Protego.

**Casting Tips:** Cast this spell with as many wizards as possible to maximize its effect.

# Quietus

**Type of Spell:** Charm

**Incantation:** KWIY-uh-tus

**Purpose:** Lowers down the volume of an object or person.

**Casting Tips:** The more you move your wand downwards while casting the spell, the lower the volume will go. This spell can be used to counter Sonorus.

# Redactum Skullus

**Type of Spell:** Hex

**Incantation:** red-AK-tum SKULL-us

**Purpose:** Shrinks the target's head.

**Casting Tips:** This spell counters Engorgio Skullus.

# Reducio

**Type of Spell:** Charm

**Incantation:** re-DOO-see-oh

**Purpose:** Shrinks an object.

**Casting Tips:** Counter to Engorgio.

# Reducto

**Type of Spell**: Curse

**Incantation**: re-DUK-toh

**Purpose**: Creates pressure inside an object causing it to break.

**Casting Tips**: If used with enough force, objects may disintegrate causing them to be unrepairable.


# Reparifors

**Type of Spell**: Healing Spell

**Incantation**: Ruh-PAIR-if-ors

**Purpose**: Heals minor ailments that were caused due to a spell such as paralysis and poisoning.

**Casting Tips**: This will also work on non-magical induced ailments.

# Relashio

**Type of Spell**: Jinx

**Incantation**: Re-LASH-ee-oh

**Purpose**: Releases someone who is bound by something physical such as a rope.

**Casting Tips**: Different wand movements are needed depending on what the binding is. For example, if it is a rope then you have to twirl your wand in a circular motion while chanting the spell.

# Rennervate

**Type of Spell**: Charm

**Incantation**: rce-nur-VAH-tay

**Purpose**: Cures paralysis from a stunned person.

**Casting Tips**: Works for both mental and physical paralysis.

# Reparifarge

**Type of Spell**: Transfiguration

**Incantation**: Ree-PAR-if-arj

**Purpose**: Reverts unsuccessful transfigurations.

**Casting Tips**: With this spell, you won't need to worry about getting a transfiguration perfect every time and will ease the pressure of learning transfiguration spells.


# Reparo

**Type of Spell**: Charm

**Incantation**: reh-PAH-ro

**Purpose**: Repairs broken object.

**Casting Tips**: Can fix objects broken by Reducto as long as they were not disintegrated.

# Repello Muggletum

**Type of Spell:** Charm

**Incantation:** reh-PELL-loh MUG-ul-tum

**Purpose:** An enchantment put on places to ward them from Muggles. Temporarily boggles their mind causing them to stray away from the warded location.

**Casting Tips:** Cast while walking around the perimeter of the location you would like to ward to maximize the area of the spell.


# Repello Inimicum

**Type of Spell:** Charm

**Incantation:** re-PEH-lloh ee-nee-MEE-cum

**Purpose:** Anyone who enters the barrier associated with this spell will be disintegrated.

**Casting Tips:** Using this along with Protego Maxima leads to a very powerful barrier.

# Revelio

**Type of Spell**: Charm

**Incantation**: reh-VEL-ee-oh

**Purpose**: Reveals hidden objects.

**Casting Tips**: This won't work on the Cloak of Invisibility but it will work on regular invisibility spells.

# Rictusempra

**Type of Spell**: Hex

**Incantation**: ric-tuhs-SEM-pra

**Purpose**: Tickles the target.

**Casting Tips**: The more you move your wand while casting the spell, the greater the tickling will be.

# Riddikulus

**Type of Spell**: Charm

**Incantation**: rih-dih-KUL-lus

**Purpose**: A spell used to combat a Boggart. Cause the Boggart to appear as whatever the caster is imagining.

**Casting Tips**: Be sure to concentrate on something you find very funny in order for this to counter the Boggart completely.


# Scourgify

**Type of Spell**: Charm

**Incantation**: SKUR-jih-fiy

**Purpose**: A cleaning spell.

**Casting Tips**: Simply point at wherever a mess is and say the spell to clean it immediately.

# Sectumsempra

**Type of Spell**: Curse

**Incantation**: sec-tum-SEMP-rah

**Purpose**: Cuts the target as if they had been slashed by a sword.

**Casting Tips**: The wand will act as the sword while chanting therefore the cut can be made based on the movement of the wand. The faster the wand is moved the stronger the cut will be.


# Serpensortia

**Type of Spell**: Conjuration

**Incantation**: ser-pen-SOR-shah

**Purpose**: Produces a snake from the tip of the wand.

**Casting Tips**: Be careful as this snake may attack you.

# Silencio

**Type of Spell:** Charm

**Incantation:** sih-LEN-see-oh

**Purpose:** Completely silences a person or animal.

**Casting Tips:** Unlike Quietus, Silencio completely silences sound rather than dulling it.

# Slugulus Erecto

**Type of Spell:** Curse

**Incantation:** Slug-YOU-luss ee-REC-toh

**Purpose:** Shoots out a green light towards the target and causes them to vomit slugs for 10 minutes.

**Casting Tips:** Be sure to point this at the right direction. Also make sure you're wand is not broken or this spell may backfire on you like it did on Ron Weasley!

# Sonorus

**Type of Spell**: Charm

**Incantation**: Soh-NOHR-us

**Purpose**: Magnifies your voice like a microphone.

**Casting Tips**: Your wand must be touching the side of your neck while talking in order to magnify your voice.


# Specialis Revelio

**Type of Spell**: Charm

**Incantation**: speh-see-AH-LIS reh-VEL-ee-oh

**Purpose**: It is said this charm causes objects such as a map or book to reveal hidden secrets.

**Casting Tips**: However, there are no recorded incidents of this spell being successful therefore it may not actually work. Find out by trying it yourself!

# Spongify

**Type of Spell:** Charm

**Incantation:** spun-JIH-fy

**Purpose:** Causes the target to soften.

**Casting Tips:** Can be used against weapons to make them harmless.


# Steleus

**Type of Spell:** Hex

**Incantation:** STÉ-lee-us

**Purpose:** Causes the victim to start sneezing temporarily.

**Casting Tips:** Great spell to distract your opponent in a duel.

# Stupefy

**Type of Spell**: Charm

**Incantation**: STOO-puh-fy

**Purpose**: Stuns the target.

**Casting Tips**: Depending on how fast the wand is swung forward, this spell can potentially knock the target unconscious.


# Taboo

**Type of Spell**: Curse

**Incantation**: tah-boo

**Purpose**: Puts a taboo on a word so that whenever that word is said by someone, their presence becomes known to the caster.

**Casting Tips**: Say the spell first then the word. Be sure it is not too common of a word or you will not be able to keep up with the amount of alarms.

# Tentaclifors

**Type of Spell**: Jinx

**Incantation**: ten-tak-liff-ors

**Purpose**: Transforms the target's head into a tentacle.

**Casting Tips**: A rather unpleasant spell that is not often used.


# Unbreakable Vow

**Type of Spell**: Binding Spell

**Incantation**: Unknown

**Purpose**: Makes a vow that one takes to be unbreakable.

**Casting Tips**: Be very careful when making a vow unbreakable because breaking it can cause death.

# Undetectable Extension

**Type of Spell**: Charm

**Incantation**: Unknown

**Purpose**: Significantly increases the capacity of a container without altering its appearance.

**Casting Tips**: Hermione may know the incantation to this spell since she has used it on her bag before.

# Ventus

**Type of Spell**: Jinx

**Incantation**: ven-TUS

**Purpose**: Blows out a blast of wind from the tip of your wand.

**Casting Tips**: The gust of wind is quite strong. It can push objects out of the way.

# Ventus Duo

**Type of Spell:** Jinx

**Incantation:** ven-TUS dew-oh

**Purpose:** A more powerful version of Ventus.

**Casting Tips:** Same as Ventus.


# Vera Verto

**Type of Spell:** Transfiguration

**Incantation:** vair-uh-VAIR-toh

**Purpose:** Transforms animals into goblets of water.

**Casting Tips:** Be sure not to drink the water!

# Verdillious

**Type of Spell**: Charm

**Incantation**: ver-DILL-eeus

**Purpose**: Shoots green sparks and flares from the tip of the wand.

**Casting Tips**: Identical to Periculum except the color of the sparks and flares.


# Verdimillious

**Type of Spell**: Charm

**Incantation**: VERD-dee-MILL-lee-us

**Purpose**: Identical to Verdillious.

**Casting Tips**: Same as Verdillious

# Verdillious Duo

**Type of Spell:** Charm

**Incantation:** ver-DILL-eeus DEW-oh

**Purpose:** A more powerful version of Verdillious.

**Casting Tips:** Same as Verdillious.


# Verdimillious Duo

**Type of Spell:** Charm

**Incantation:** VERD-dee-MILL-lee-us DEW-oh

**Purpose:** A more powerful version of Verdimillious.

**Casting Tips:** Same as Verdimillious.

# Vipera Evanesca

**Type of Spell:** Untransfiguration

**Incantation:** VIYP-er-uh ehv-uhn-EHS-kuh

**Purpose:** Counters Serpensortia. Disintegrates the snake.

**Casting Tips:** This only works for snakes summoned by Serpensortia, not regular snakes.

# Vulnera Sanentur

**Type of Spell:** Healing Spell

**Incantation:** vul-nur-ah sahn-en-tur

**Purpose:** Heals cuts and gashes including returning blood to the victim.

**Casting Tips:** Works great against Sectumsempra.

# Waddiwasi

**Type of Spell:** Charm

**Incantation:** wah-dee-WAH-see

**Purpose:** Throws small objects in the air.

**Casting Tips:** Can be used only for small objects.
Swipe with your wand in the direction that you want the
object to go.

# Wash the Dishes

**Type of Spell:** Charm

**Incantation:** Unknown

**Purpose:** Enchants dirty dishes to wash themselves.

**Casting Tips:** The incantation is unknown but Molly
Weasley probably knows it!

# Wingardium Leviosa

**Type of Spell:** Charm

**Incantation:** win-GAR-dee-um lev-ee-OH-sa

**Purpose:** Used to levitate and move a target.

**Casting Tips:** Use your wand to direct the movement of the target.

180 Spells from the Wizarding World of Harry Potter to help you become a Master Wizard or Witch today.

ISBN 9781731544872